Private Information:

A poetry and Prose collection

©2021 Joshua T. Wells.

First Print Edition, 2019, United States of America.
Second Print Edition, 2020, United States of America.
Third Print Edition, 2021 United States of America.

ISBN 978-1673711219
        979-8584812690

LCCN 95830576128

Private Information: A Poetry and Prose Collection©2021 Joshua Wells.
All information presented in this book is a product of the author's imagination and does not refer to real people or events.

IG @iCyddlyfe.n.inks

Email: Capncydd@gmail.com

IV

CONTENTS

Private Information:
A poetry and Prose collection

Joshua T. Wells

JOSHUA TIMOTHY WELLS

" Someone smells storms in your eyes; and all you can do is live in mercy against the sea."

JOSHUA TIMOTHY WELLS

AS IT FALLS

Have you ever looked deep across the night sky wondering
as it starts falling, could you hold the weight?

With only two hands shaking every corner of our planet felt
deep within our souls. This feeling twists a stomach inside out.

"I will be okay."

It's all you have to say.

THAT DAY

One day I just gave up loving anyone. I loved myself,
and that was enough.

I learned to love the Earth. Feeling the dirt and air.

Water as it moved through my hands.

My pulse; in it's ups and downs as time would pass.

I became a fisherman at peace understanding Hemingway's tale

"The Old Man and the Sea."

A love for life among light stood unchallenged; and
you called my bluff as Earth itself slipped away.

MUTINY

You put value on me; and speak of friends with a red coat and
a knife in your pocket. What have you done for me? Stab. Stab.
Stab. I'll ask again, what will you do for me? It's a question with
intention. An intention you cannot give in a lack of attention.
When I start chasing the satire of our game, and the mutiny
shows in the crimson stains, across crimson sheets of paper once
white. How do you intend to prove it's more then just irony?

CHAOS

I've never had more fun watching my body break
and grenades fling while pins fall. Burning imaginary
fleets and sewing death on sheets.

Floating high enough to feel a rage and make
peace with a disbelief in stolen Gods.

Days have passed, and I am neck deep. Battlefields
becoming insanity. A haze building a cacophony of
plague; and I have succumbed to wicked ideas.

Holding far to high this chaotic mind and its twisted thoughts.
I dive through mental torment and thunder like a stunned
corpse. I land in gravel stone and break another round of bones.

A heavy jaw that cannot speak overwhelms what remains. A
lazy eye that loses focus while I roam endlessly through hell.

Is there any solid ground to be found? Nope, just a sober and
loaded gun. A grin of losing yourself in sin as chaos begins.

BEAUTIFUL

Weeks pass alone spent salted by sand and clay. Northeastern winter gales blow endlessly across an aging sea. It cuts deep into cold blue flesh nightly from dark and distant hills.

These long nights I've known never end. I have grown at ease with what I know of her depths and wicked little machines.

Haunted by spirits of the Pacific Southwest.
Here before I rest, I listen;

Hear them chanting, singing, and summoning. A foreign language drifts across my thoughts.

Summer has come, and gone and here again when the wind is still. The suns fury claims itself wild without chains.

Golden death pours across these valleys and hills. It leathers the flesh and kills without remorse. Perhaps how the spirits and shadows that wander here greeted their unwilling death.

Alive and formed, they manifest tonight at my side.
Through the hills they whisper and speak.

DECLINE

I lay my head below rock and stone to sleep in peace.
Comforted only by the dying embers of a youthful flame.

Dim light remains' and I lift my eyes across another sea. The
clear sky in my corner of the Earth tonight. Ten million strong
or more, an endless ocean hung overhead awoke a short few
hours ago. Its colors strewn in all directions; A timeless beauty
has found me humbled underneath a moonless night.

North to South her heart runs like a river shimmering in dust
clouds. The bright cosmic plain. While Sagittarius pulses
at her center. A constellation, and further still a black hole
in the darkness. Her hunger has no care of human flight.

An abyssal maw that swallows all thought. Their secrets
draw my curiosity to the point of no return.
Louder the spirits chant and sing;

"Closer, closer..."

They cast their spells upon the winds and her gaze focuses below.

Incantations drawing presence in my own pulse. The whispers
pass through veins and bones, an echo... "Home."

THEATER OF SECRETS

I learned one of those trade secrets last night. I don't know how many times it took to learn. Love is no secret at all! It's poetry to the soul! It makes you shout hallelujah. It finds you dreaming; and hallucinating an ink full of poetry fed in the silence of the joyful soul. I've been subdued by the company of what it taught me to keep in privacy; and I shout the answers when I find them. I hear that sound of battleships across the theater of stars; and I admit these notes fold into a story of our fathers wars. Even greater imagination has formed in that sound. My fathers war is already won.

FLAME FORGED

Overheating melting iron arcing a soul that died
in the wind. Shouts and burdens explode.

Flowing fire from a waterfall. Inward into the flames I fold.

Wounded by my own foul breath.

Savage laughter buries the spells that weave a raw mold.

Smoking embers thrown like kindling over coal. Flames soar
pulled into the air above. Mental instability suffocates the oxygen. Iron and carbon melt into steel. At this rate, unbreakable.

You fuel suffocation, pestilence, and plague.

None of which are my ways. I'm willing to
die in flames forging steel veins.

While burying the coals until diamonds appear -

They'll fall like rain unearthed from the
dark side of a living forge.

SMOKE

Anger's taken its noose and I am set on freedom or
death. Withering in curses turning loose an animal of
man who breaks in half-howling at moonlight.

While fires stretch across my eyes and forms jaded stones of ruby
light. Blood calls to the painful fury of endless smoke taking hold.

Over a decade the black ink cast spells to summon
dragons into flight across smoke and horizons.

Nightmares and black sickness dwells in him now.

The cacophony of raw rage forms these hallucinations in
my eyes. A maddening sense of smoke within oneself. That
painful blow stirred the fiery haze where sight re-awoke.

VISITORS

All these shades of pitch and tar. Crawling
on walls, and across my skin.

My nightly guests becoming a summoned ritual.

A remembrance of another life.

While their haunting voices fill this room with gallows
grip and a strangling soup.

Sanity where did I lose you this time.

Gravity pulls on the heavy, sinking, limping frame.

Blinded by flickering starlight bright as day as it swallows sight.

Day turns black like a photo negative paralyzing
every step of tired, and lead lined legs.

Relentless, the dead are set to stake a claim on what is dying. I
am succumbing to the swarm crawling through the windows.
Drowning all light and sound as I slip into these visitor's names.

SCHIZOPHRENIA

The blood red glowing gaze of that shadow haunts me. Staring and reaching within ethereal claws. As my hand is pressed into the deepest cold touch this body has ever known; and with it a thousand echoes roared in the darkness. These voices will soon fade, and the shadows haunting display melts and dissipates.

Death himself I fear has come to know me by name. It found a way through trap doors and battle scars into depths of a human heart.

The curse of man has awoken in me; and the maw of jagged, and sharpened teeth stirs below my feet. The blurring line of reality has come to wrestle with his faith. An emotional swarm of pain; and madness manifests beside a free mind. I am lost in the air, and swelling smells of pine.

I say to it;

"Madness my dark, and dearest friend! It's been awhile, but I am here for you to take if heaven has given you my name."

WICKED DREAMS

While demons in the darkest corner of the maw stir in their
excitement of a soul filled feast. An emblazoned spirit begins
its descent into that war. A scar that hides it's toxic venting.
I have been battle hardened by the world's deep and blue
across the cosmos. The minds' disease that I have trespassed.
Worlds high; and found joyful of red soaked sands awoke.

Through a widow's web my mind has woven what
it learns of illness. I believe there is no escape
to this plight taking a grip on my life.

THROUGH THE DARK

Daydreaming in darkness until sparks begin. Your eyes settle
behind my blind; broken right squinting in the sun.

Now all I have is constellations forming in the rubble,
replacing you. The same eye that woke darkened
fills with a silent wicked love.

Play with fire as it burns like stars. Sit silent in
an education for crowns as all the others do. In
time, you'll see that pit consume you.

Play with fire, and greet the devil who has tricked
you into his game of false beliefs.

Now I am like you.

I see the corners of my eyes in ways of losing faith;
and only time will tell if I am meant to lose it.

I am tongue tied as I drown in an uncontrollable
flame designed to replace what I cling too.

BURNED ALIVE

Another war. Another night like all the others come
before. You would think I'd have learned by now. Instead
this thick tarred blood recedes. I choose not to die in
flames. I have a choice. to die lost in planets and stars.

Is it worse than childbirth to be reborn through
a darkness and rise a Phoenix; Until we see the
way the light shines through the trees?

I resist budging and reinforce the walls built
with another layer of bone –

"Damned if I break down one more time. It happens all
the time." I say in some cliché way. I suffocate.

I tremble and gasp fighting a cancerous grasp on my soul.
Shaking these nerves back to life for simpler things. These
flames leave an enraged imprint as they divide in the ashes
of the mind. These emotions become just to much ripping
and chewing at swollen lungs; and choking on the blood.

Silence my tongue and stand strong by the faith. I
choose, and the storm will come. I will still say;

"Just another demon knocking at the door becoming
a demon. I ignore."

COFFINS

Building coffins now until wood turns to glass. Payments in blood for the past, to watch a garden grow. I will wait patiently six feet below wandering the mind's eye rabbit holes.

"You'll wake a vampire."

The wood creaked and moaned.

"One with a thirst for thicker blood.

No satisfaction from wine alone."

Back and forth I turn to feel every little note; and does it matter anymore to lose touch with the real world?

This stiff grip has come to rewrite death and stir a sober mind. One that knows the value of light. The power to kick the shadows from a soul's home.

I see this life through two hearts in the same bones. The dead and living both bloom. I am clear as glass knowing the stories I have heard describe these things. I find this logic lawless.

Yet real in a window where a fresh breeze begins to blow; and all these little notes become a coffin full of midnight thoughts with nowhere to go.

MEN

All I hear anymore is talk of aliens and viruses; and the talk
just goes on and on into circles while I try to understand
the word by being a good man. My bible says they do not
exist but it certainly paves a way for the best form of Men.
Although it says not a single one; All I do is join the talk
of aliens and viruses best drank with a side of lime.

The lip service finally moves on; and I find reality right
where I left it. Even the chaos, and the messiest sides
remain unchanged. Although something is changing; and
I hear no talk of drunks from aliens and lime disease.

TAKING FLIGHT

Round and round my pillow turns as a stomach burns.
A heavy whisper that lifts a distant hurt. Through all
the years of intoxicated dives. I find night flights, and
reaching into a sober mind strong enough to see and feel
its belief. You have been here; You have seen them all.

Remember the younger days? Simple seeds. Saplings
weaving roots into the oceans we've become today. Now
you are a beautiful rose I must cast into the flames.

Your early flights caught my eye. My memory still
feels them like thorns. You were awestruck; and
that awe has inspired this life I chose.

Now to see this through. Go full circle.

We are at our demise falling far from each other's
shores. Years have gone by for you. Leaving our marks
on what we knew was something simpler.

If you believe the words you spoke. I believe you'll fall
safely in the arms of where you are meant to go.

I will do the same, wherever my own story goes.

VOYAGES

Every notebook has become a voyage named memory.
Aging slowly with barnacles and salty seas. They speak of
compasses, and time star charts predetermined destinies.

They are brigantines of paper set to sail amongst the changing
tides. They become maps themselves set to stand the test of
time. I will allow cannons to be set against the darkness of
tomorrow. Through explosive shots in the sounds of naval war.
Set wrongs to right as I live by the sword, and by pen. These pages
will turn full sail ahead into the night. Filling it with nightmares
of creative space through paper. I am beginning to believe.

If that belief is right. The past has finally become the wreckage
of a ship deep below. This flag will stand high. Unyielding in its
natural course these notes will pay no tribute to unjust kings.

Port to port I've sailed; and counted the memories
with the best of crews. Who I have witnessed losing
everything Through watery graves.

Whatever the reasons may be. Maelstroms, monsoons or
ebb and flow of tides. Perhaps mutiny by keg and powder
gone wrong. They have simply sunk or sailed.

In my remorse. I know where these sails have been.

Those icy cold depths are calling my name. The treasures
and secrets survive in the holds. I have my doubts but into
the cold this vessel will go. A passing sailors' tale I will tell
and retell, about mastering a ship. If you can believe in such
impossible things. We are all voyagers searching for a home.

BLACK ILLUSION

I find shadows; and dancing in silhouettes. Glowing in candles set upon the sails.

A sense of magic lingering in these frozen illusions.

Wearing black velvet. Speaking through cosmic dreams across starry nights with a black and cold moon. Into the papers shadow stretched across a blank page.

Hello, black velvet silhouette. Darling, wear your shadows as they are elusive hues across the illusions.

DEEP

You'll find your puzzle when you start exploring the deep. It's never dark where the stars fell, just look up. As though death was not on their to-do list; and I will hold the keys to my own secrets, and my own cosmos. I am certain I am leaving solid ground in the past now to find a peace of mind. That was well earned.

Through the broken hourglass of endlessly falling sands of pandora's box. I began collecting time through toe-taps and guitar strings. Emotions are nothing more then moving images across a public space; and a sound wave that soothes the bleeding headache.

Once my eyes find these puzzles in everything being uprooted between scales molt and feathered thoughts. I have begun sleep-ing nightly with a sense of quantum mechanics ticking away just over my head. Passing through like solar flares in sun charred hair.

I've begun to hide my dreams; and I begin to think in deeper depths. Emotional interstellar clouds. Stirring puzzles in my own hourglass. Spilling sand to bury what has come and gone.

MACHINES

Deeper still my intentions have been set on this head trip.
The pen and note answer once again. Right through the
scars of a ravaging mental illness that claims what has
become of me. As though I am nothing more then a circling
machine. I am running the gauntlet of Drake's Passage.

Right through the cold seas I have come close to fathoming
a true sense of deep. Somewhere in this mind's eye. The sun
hangs low; and skin turns blue at the sea's sharp bite.

This long trip across the southern skies I've never
seen before. It seems I am not getting it right. As it
keeps spinning round back into my sight.

I'll do it again and again. Until the lesson I may never learn
has settled. Survival is a funny thing when Earth slips away
under your own feet. The growing sobriety leaves a sharp
scar on a mind learning it's need for truth and reasoning.

DROWNED OUT

All my senses of reality have drowned searching for a way out of this sea. An ocean of madness that has swallowed my path to solid ground, while asking the mirror to give up on myself. I could cut my losses and return to who I once knew. How could I give up on a war that started the other day to save this spinning soul?

Truth needs to be exposed, and this pen is speaking of a way. This started as a child staring out of windows at the monsters and things so much worse. Those faces in the glass that did not exist at all. They still haunt pieces of who I am today. I tried to drink it out, but there is never enough to drown out the way they swim around in a sea of alcohol. Back and forth fighting between two minds. All these thoughts, all these feelings, leading him into a finger pointing game at the voices laughing at it all.

I will admit to being in this alone while I laugh at the pain being devoured by joy of scribbles on a wall. Humbled by a crown that comes through overworking a mind caught in nets and noose.

DITCH THE SEA

The sea is clear. The sky is calm. Turn back to reality.
Is there is a way? Reality for him is barely held by
bleeding wires. The clouds looming in his brain.

I will tell him.

"Believe, this will be a healing memory."

The air is creeping in and touching skin reminds me of
a way to be free. It will be real. The waves finally pass
over; and it no longer storms when ditching the sea.

FLOOD

A river forms from a full moon becoming
a flood across the desert.

Nearly summer; and the night is cooling. Soothing
to an aching sunburn.

Feels as though I am calling Earth my home
soon as the season begins.

As I sit back and watch a river of black ink becoming
a flood resembling a full moon across a desert.

Words float, and spiral from that face we have seen.
Words that stretch into the milky way.

As they touch Earth, becoming the magic of her heart
and her soul. I sense something in this flood.

A twisted clamp on the spine piercing deep that I must
believe in strange things becoming reality.

An illusion of floods and words alike, both made
hollow. I see the flood overtaking the remains.

THE BOTTOM

I carve my name at the base of a glaciated stem. I try
to turn away and face another crushing wave of Earth
and snowfall. The mudslides through memory, and
followed by the electric jolts of my own stupidity.

I've seen too many things to waste these fool hearted
dreams of my own disease. Where mountains rise
cascading downward through my false eye.

I am left, in the cold arctic breeze blowing through my
soul. Though I am alive; and no one seems to know the way
sin destroys. I show all the signs of bleeding and crippled
thinking. There is an avalanche coming down to bury this
place at the bottom of the Earth. At the bottom of a sea.

When it's over I'll be climbing over icy walls across my
brain. My numb senses weakened in overloads of cold.

When it's over I'll be begging my legs to sprout
roots and drink a deeper well of the Earth.

A SINKING SHIP

Carving out the wooden ribs of this sinking brig. Searching for the soul you tried to claim. I dream of freedom without anchors into feeling everything you believe. When another captain fights for your wheel. is he swearing, he'll be going down with the ship. Before he turns back before he meets wet sails. Think of me. I'll already be the brig at the bottom of the sea. Free.

Find me then where thunder howls across the dark dead waters. Where the lightning is red; and the Earth moves across the desert. I will be long gone and breathing in warm rising air. I will be looking across the night sky to tell a wandering eye I only believe in what I see.

So lay your curses at the bottom of your own sea; and you will learn how a man breaks free. Devouring his own dreams. There is a strange sense developing in these notes. Drawing deeper emotions into reality. A sense of the sea becoming thin as air at the edge of space. Bad or good, I live here in these.

GROUND ZERO

I break, I twist and tear at them coming apart while the bones that fueled them become dust. Until I am finger painting in clear water. In the shadows of stars. The years cross his face and the war we waged is ending. I never want a garden that looks like yours and how you destroy such beautiful things by fears. Instead of carrying it with faith.

I promise truth and keep it safe and as it bleeds the soul. I will soon claim both in my sleep at the bottom of her soul.

EXPOSING THE HULL

A ship of bones shows no signs of relief; and a party in my head
has filled with the dead. Ready for that arctic glow. The cold
chill of another blow of growing alone. Silence has healed
the aching wound and the echoing door has sealed two. The
storm has evolved into something I cannot control with a
hand on Earth; and I will never wonder why faith is purpose
after this storm. Sound has become more then hollow stock
in a ships hold. The cold winds stir and blow. I've learned now
to not mind it in the bones. Though I am impatient for the
whisper and the blending fire with powder against the tides.
Old names just flash in that pan; and even in ice I've learned
a way to keep the cannons dry. I tried to deny thunder and
light. As I was taking the helm of the captain in my eyes.
Although I was only doomed to be a ship

of bones at the end of life.

EATING WATER

Salts become a weapon and it stains black and red across her face.

I am eating her waters, feeling gravity taking over my feet.

Holding this broken thing together for you.

One day at a time as I begin to understand what is happening.

While I bleed from my palms until it looks like stardust
tricking from meteor showers.

Drawing nude beaches across her sheets.

We are building sandcastles to hide ourselves from sight.

Whatever it takes to sooth the blues.

We are eating water with a periscope view of a cosmic collision.

Searching for another chapter in this story about you.

A new answer to the rise and fall of the moon.

How many ways can love bleed and shape
new colors in her magic?

A kaleidoscope through heartaches drained away.

Filling the hungry belly with water.

I've paid a price eating up the blue, you've
paid drinking up the red.

Let's call this a collision creating stars. we
share waking in the night.

Let's call this eating water, and...

DRINKING FIRE

Drinking fires in reborn eyes.

Drinking straight through circles in a supernova of desire.

Let me drink what I taste in you.

Drunk on the flames, and I am listening to you in wave and wire.

Everything you think is pure and blinding desire.

Liquid and molten bodies raw enough to break.

You and I are melting into the fires.

When did I start dreaming these things?

Miracles becoming real as hands flow across skins embrace.

You smell like sulfur and highs from an evil place.

A freedom drunk from flames over molten ice.

You smell like love and death in paradise.

Like rug burns and bad poetry that cannot
come close to being drunk in fires.

OUTER REACH

Saturn from angel wings. Stone hearts and dead deeds.

Broken resistance.

Broken greed.

Rushing water.

Rushing breeze.

Translations that form rings.

Never a reply through windows speech.

Neptune hums a hymn to deepest sleep. Ears bleed cold cacophony in perfect harmony. Venus wakes from the grave of a fiery sea. A phoenix aloud to breath.

An Aphrodite when wires break, and men fall into the sea. Through alien atmospheres in soundscapes. Her control of the mind's eye through purest lies.

Slipping into broken discord, tallest silent heights. She sighs in the cold outer reach. Stone hearted. Stone spirited. The voice fades in the transactions paid through fire and ice. A voice, I never wanted to hear at all.

CURVATURES

Endless waves motion.

Brought to orbit.

Three simple words.

Crested from undertows.

Astral flow.

Energetic soul.

Tethers release.

Gentle Alchemy.

Secrets known.

Shining gold.

Auroral glow.

Spirit life.

Lost minds.

Your eyes.

GLOW

Nightmares bring shadows.
But shadows bring light.
Neon monsters.
The comforts of ionized atmospheric light.

Seven days I ran without sleep.
Seven more I thought I was lost daily.
Seven days in her glow.

Pressurized scars run deep.
They burn roots locked in lungs.
Embers in spinning smoke.
Anxious stomachs groan.
Neon nightmares sewn.

A pillow's voice echoed –
"I don't know who you're talking too."
As if I was using my voice –
Still I reply, "not you."
With a bird's salute, to no one at all.

WELDED

Electrical arcs.

Explosive chaff flutters to life.

Inward towards the flames.

Another round inside the forge.

Maybe it was nickel.

Sparks caught my hand on fire.

My own savage laughter to burn flesh like kindling over coal.

In body shapes of iron and nickel.

Through bones radon overdose.

Maybe it was oxygen.

Maybe it was acetylene.

All I know is that forge, was too damn cold.

BALANCE

Pitch a tent inside my brain and build a campfire to
hold back the cold. One that stays while he learns
to ignore the rain filling another ocean.

He has learned a few things about salvaging from
the depths of the Marianas trench.

The pain involved is real.

A price to fuse the pieces together that mix; and learn to love the
parts that do not. Do you know how cold the water gets though?

I don't know if it's easier to be a tent or house, but
it takes a little of both to build a home.

TANTRUMS

I won't stay in a cage rusting away.

I won't be stepping back either.

I'll find a better way and move around your tantrum today.

Kindly carve you out.

While you spill idle nonsense.

Staring between white spaces.

Blue lines to fill with light.

From those cursed flames.

That fill your mind with open skies.

To ease the pain of living life.

You learn to lie and hide certain things.

Through those lies you found a better life.

Ash becomes snow-like in time.

Those windows close and you stay inside.

Black ink and blood spill instead. Across blue lines,
white space and fill them with depth and light.

As I say; "I love the tantrum you throw tonight."

HYDRA

My emotions dwell in shapes of a hydra living on mountain
peaks by day, and neon reapers grinning in evil haze through
nights. I have become both. With all this noise whispering
this way and the other. Trying to sleep with star dust
and frost bite fluttering in the monotony of my insanity.
Leaving something behind in the scars to say I was real. I
had dreams I could never reach becomes maddening.

I've wandered into the thickets and the brambles of Eden. An
explosion of life at the thought. An overgrowth through thrill
after thrill, day after day. Anxiety just primes the charge before
the lightning strike of dead emotions surge an anchored depth.
Another dust cloud to clear out keeping me awake. I must tell
myself she brings an army of crazy with her; and I will not be
telling her how she resembles a hydra more then medusa.

My beating blood cannot escape the nervous twitch
in my eye. All the anxious looks I see on faces sensing a
hearts ethereal heat. In her defense, she did wake my eyes
to Eden and not the land of the dead. This time.

EDEN

Is it Eden where I woke yesterday? With you ready to fight and
I am ready to speak. Vines, and palms grow beautifully; and
creatures here all stir without a fear of man. Far beyond the fires
and the seas. I believe I feel like I've spent years in Eden already.

I am aware there is a curse woven among the veins of this land.
A chance we will not be allowed to stay. We are castaways
here. Our spirits lost among the starlit nights. They whisper
beauty through the trees, and show images of another world
we all left behind. Sapphire skies filled with diamond dust
and cold fresh air through winter nights. The smell of a star
filled sea fills my nose with what is pouring out of you.

You have driven him to the depths, and brought him
through the highs of this wild belief. You believed;
and now, I must say, I do too.

STARS

This is where the stars open their fiery hearts. Under the sea they churn, between belly, and lung. I am breathing fine now. I hold ground in everything I touch. Enough of myself in this star lined heart; these sparks awoke for you.

Will you shake the eye from the depths of the Earth? Will you feel the breeze pull you up and hold you close to the moon? She'll pull you into her breathe and show you even bigger views.

When the sky above flashes black one more time in broad daylight. One more day to hang on, and take control of who you are and not they are.

When you wrestle with am I God or just another devil? You are a creator, and nothing more. Gifted to turn everything handed to you into something more.

You have magic at the wave of your hand. It will turn the gaze of a universe from the depths of the sea upon you. Take the stars you've been given and throw them across the black sky you found in broad daylight.

- A letter to a future divided self.

VIRGO

I am exploring the galaxy clusters in my constellation until I know every single one; and every secret they hold close. Hidden in the shelter of words, or actions, I hope they are noble. As smiles form again remembering who, and what still exists in life.

A quiet place to sooth the weary soul and the open mind that feels itself. Breathing the air on a limb keeping toys close and eyes closed. Roaming the desert watching Jupiter pass through Virgo as I become who I intended to be.

NEPTUNE

I feeling you singing a subtle pull.

A synaptic lens opened by your half-in,
half-out lingering presence.

Enough to keep me awake through the night.

Are you parading just another Siren's song?

One that pulls him into even darker depths.

Endless cold blue atmospheres,

A howling tension through an icy wall; and a crumbling
that knows no end.

Or is it all just lies again?

You smell of them.

I found freedom here in the center of a storm.

An art seeing through darkness.

Are we prisoners of gravity ... of a storm?

Or have we given ourselves thoroughly to him?

My dear, don't you know at all, I was never captive by you.

I already gave myself to a King above.

LADIES FIRST

Drill if you must while war drums fill this cold ringing night.

Let's greet fire at dawn, when our own sun dims.

Ladies first.

This crown you placed has worn thin. Now
that the water has grown so clear.

While his core spins new motion, and avoids wandering
into the devil's palm before the stars exhale fresh air.

My dear, the oceans might and depth hasn't had enough of us.

Bodies have been left broken by our war. They cascade
like waterfalls in this dream of other worlds.

Ladies first.

I'll dive right behind you, as I always have while I hide and brood.

Maybe, he'll sing to the rhythm of a war drum as he
is snared in thorn roots blindly untangling his own.
Slipping away, slowly, fires still roar and bridge the open
sea. Now I know the bridges don't burn into you.

JUPITER

The dead have risen, and the cold has conquered
whatever home I still recognize.

It's not new anymore to lose everything,
to be made clean and new.

The man I've become has lost his taste for steel and blood.

Perhaps today I will lay down joining the shallow graves.

Lock me in a hold. Let Jupiter's pull take over!

Leave these words dead, and cold in the past where we met light.

Felt it through paying my dues to stars; and holding
a night sky in my hands.

I'll wage open war on darkness; and the creatures
that stir in the chop.

I will slip away into a storm stretching this imagination
into bubbled confetti.

Colorful, yet cold sad meandering notes until
I find an absolute cold bitter truth.

I have few words left of this cold place, but I have found faith.

MARS

Mars has all gone mad. A bloodied back and forth war among fools. Little green men crawl, and the shadows stand eight feet tall. As if molten radon vibrates with reason while waging cosmic war on liquid rock.

Go back home and sink below this starry-eyed sea. I have tried as toxic vents of cosmic downpours yield an exile of high altitude, and lost aptitude. A dive deeper than any Earth binding sea has opened red scars; and turned her into nothing more than a glass doll. Men are from Mars is all I can think.

I believe in ancient glows found among lava flows. Indigo skies, and endless stars on the darkest night; singing about a home we will never reach. Not this ancient rusting rock among our warring souls. Anchored without logic answering questions. You become nothing more than shadows at war.

Mars has all gone mad; and I am not immune to suffering at the hands of his madness. I crumble through walls, but now I know you'll never pierce a veil casting silent stones.

EARTH

Watch thundering jaws roar then wage war. Colony by colony.
Just a blue ball full of fire ants scurrying around searching
for meals, and searching for slaves. Anything to get ahead
and unleash their vile venom. Anything it seems to show
their toxic sting. Anything that alleviates their pain.

That giant white light of gas above will someday destroy
them all. They fear death, they fear losing wagers, and worse
losing their souls. Screaming for salvation has taught me
something. It does not exist in books. (Oh, how wrong I was)

Here I am playing my own cursed God pointing a lens at fire
ants hoping pressure and heat will satisfy my needs. I broke
myself again in my own expanding thoughts. They were more
than surface projections with a venomous anger in words.

With fire and lenses of illusionary wars. My hearts drum
synchronized with loud, cosmic, and starry vapors. White
cold ash and snow has lost its place inside these bones.
I'll be diving back into that blue ball soon with a deeper,
finer tuned love, and letting her lens burn him up.

PLUTO

Bring a plague as I cross the cold vastness of space in a year that never seems to end. I never find a goodbye that reaches my soul. I feel lost between Olympus and Earth in this cold place.

A heartbreak that tore my world in two. Silent death putrified blood so rank it toxifies the air for all to see.

Blindness and polarized lenses hide this irrational thinking for weeks. They reflect a green glowing haze pouring from some celestial instinct trickling through a maze.

An overdose on pain met sympathy; and found apathy in wandering to close to a dividing sensory. Broken, and real, I believe you know exactly what I feel as I wander this lonely place.

I pay my coin to Charon in welcoming arms to Hades. I am paying for the soul I want returned to me. I want to recover from this. I'll ask Pluto once I cross the river Styx for a return on his investment. The feeling pulling me deeper and closer in the darkness of that shoreline. I remember even Pluto answers to a greater king. Now this challenge is laid in stone, and a goal made to retrace the way I came.

GALAXIES

Ten million projects before death is a dream worth projecting.
One by one I feel the pipes inside the frames are laid. I see
the depth of blooming eyes. I love the sound they make
at night. Get me through reality when the desert sun has
no mercy. The cold inside holds sturdy and I taste those
calm waters. You'll have lifetimes with me before death
claims anything less then the millions of dreams. That is
the path laid out ahead. I have faith it'll be a good ride.

Ten million stars is on my list before fading into the eve of a
setting sun. Built by a hull of iron repeated a million times.
Nine million more to go is no surprise. I'll waste those falling in
love and waste nothing when Autumn brings a cooling sun.

WANDERER

Shapeshifting quantum theories into realities. Into
points of light, and little dots of dust fluttering. Burning
eyes like dead stars choking on iron. Am I about to pop?
I sense another mirror hiding in the cosmic darkness
through ripples of time floating down Styx.

I watched a hydra and a titan wage war months ago. I closed that
wound, and then ran molten across a lover's sky. Blind half a day
staring into a blur through the other half. I came back a wanderer
holding tighter this faith-fueled truth. I became kinetic energy
and flashbacks of Vietnam jungles brought forth more terror.
A place I've never seen, and in truth, never wish to see again.

While rattling the brain like an oven-baked pig on a spit. This is
a fire to destroy, snuff out and; forget faith exists. Darkness has
crawled into my bed and hid the meteor showers overhead. My
eyes are being vaporized by the cosmic water line I continually
tread. Searching the darkness now for colors and exo-planets. I
believe even the lifeless must be better than this terror. Nebulous
star birth should be moving in and through his skin. I need out of
this suit of flesh. Let me stretch myself across the Earth again.

MY WORLD

Between darkness and never knowing where I am. Faith
has presence. Sleeping or walking both the same thing;
and they tell me I can feel you coming around.

I've ran out of dreams through the night, so I started watching
them through the day with open eyes, and other minds. I run to
keep my hands mine and in control of the white and blue lines.

If it's all I can keep for myself will it ever stop trembling?
When I don't even recognize my own darkness,
and cannot admit I am vulnerable.

The man in my eyes wandered its way into death. Time has
brought sobriety creeping ever closer in this life. I have been de-
voting myself to the notion God exists and Jesus is a true savior.

I smell the fear of an unknown in all of it. I see flying objects,
silver, and shiny across the hills. As mythologies come to life.

Let me keep my hand. Let me hide in it; and claim the
rest of my life through the faith I will continually admit.
Jesus is alive. The crazy depths grow crazier, and maybe
it's a mid-life crisis or is it finally true faith persists?

COLORS

Turn back around; and wave goodbye to translucent dreams.
The planets have long drifted out of my minds orbit. I never
see them anymore as I once did. No longer living brain dead.

All the chirping distractions. These auroral realities
that will someday be home to colorful ink.

I must bite my tongue and laugh at nightmares, the broken
thoughts; and all my failures that lead me to this colorful existence. Every pen stroke I feel the tension, the strain of breaking
cords to an old dead child. I am a blind man lost in the black and
white. I'm awake more then I sleep today. I found a color exists
in that. Reality could slip under the floor again into the clouds of
mental golden vapors as it has before but I am awake to watch it.

Weightless thoughts encounter daybreak. Color
across the Earth, and stretching arms in the morning
glow. I feel it. Fire without the devil's breath.

This colorful sense as I stare at floors lately calling
it stargazing to where I have been. I stare at ceilings
wondering why everything has grown so silent.

EMPTY HANDS

I search still through the coal and carbon of yesterday for
whatever I may have missed. The past looks more like
a black hole into an empty abyss of an empty life.

An emptiness never filled with witchcraft and pentagram
nonsense. Deep into the Earth I've found more then prisms and
colorful diamonds that brought these fruits into existence.

I have measured and weighed the full spectrum
of color I found in this living place.

ANTI-GRAVITY

The Earth still trembles when my knees give way.
Today solid roots hold me in place. I close my eyes,
and look up listening to the clouds paint a story as
the rain silences the cosmos in my mind.

I wait to connect the dots and draw lines across the sky digging
deeper into the meaning of weightlessness. There is a history
in these beautiful sights handed down from ancient man. Plato
and Aristotle, or the first sea bound explorers navigating by
the solar winds we call light. Full sail has come over me; and
reality is drawing lines. Making star charts to understand
why the black ink has taken such importance in my life.

I make my own maps across this plain white space open
to the oblivion of the darkness above. I am becoming
the edge of my own universe as I crumble into the
floor and cry for safety, occasionally.

Shipwrecked in silence through an overload of mental color
and anti-gravitic notions. My hands fold watching this world
with a closer eye on the faith I find in transfigured parts.

I have learned to resist the rusted cog effect; and defy gravity,
just enough to get on my knees and pray to a God I know exists.

SUNSETS

Watching a sunset through pastel paint. Orange, and
pink scattered in the darkening clouds. A little light
left fading to the glow of the moon. Old pain resurfaced
today. Old notes, and an old fortress showed in my eyes
where the sky cracked in two. Things I've relived for over
a decade is not new, yet a beauty shine's through.

I can remember the old worlds we created to run away into
still hidden in the recesses of the mind. Someday sunset
will come and claim this aging body between here and
heaven whispering how I lived this life. The way I chased
the moon across the stars at the summit of mountain
peaks. That sunset is still the same old image despite how
we adjusted our view to fit a faith into an old frame.

The constant ticking of heartache has never changed its pitch;
and for that I am grateful recovery will be found before our
last sunset. It's a reminder of being nothing more then human
carrying a tick-tock way of moving forward. The paper-thin view
of my world is setting tonight and in it I lay down my crutches to
wake in a fresh dawn. Refocused in a light that changed my view.

HERESY

Before they cry heresy as he watches biblical notions burn. I will rest my past in these new dark ages; confess what I have done to be a heretic through the noise of and bellows of a tinted moon.

They'll cast it upon you in their beds fast asleep. Weaving dreams that do not fit their own boots. Men with crowns who never test the gold of fools. They no longer realize the breadth of the world they claim to own. Lost in the constant aching blood stain from the cup pressed upon their lips. I bleed my heresy biting more then I can chew in a crippling loss of senses. The day is coming we will be reborn something new. That promise stands true.

Until that day I wait, and play God weaving spells into the air. I am weaving a way out of this war I waged on thin air. In this land I have cried heresy on myself. I walk away this time alone into the road of a martyr. A heretic's grave. This black ink spilled will be the concrete and mortar of the life I changed.

BRANDED

Slipping through dark needs once more. Tar-stained fingers show water marks of mistakes. Burdens that line a heavy heart in my stomach. Burning and folding deeper within itself turns a good man into a lost cause slipping through his own branded beliefs. Snow has finally begun to melt and summer is showing itself. Six months of sanity held crashing on the rock they call Jesus. This sunken heart has searched every corner of a wasteland for what it means to be, like, Christ.

This heart has become branded by a cause to find stars in places others never dared to search. To find the Sun and Moon giving blessing to those who need it the most. I finally see an image of myself as both a beast of darkness and a heart that evaporates at the sight of blood. I savored a feast stolen before I could even enjoy the taste of its delicacy on my lips. Every smell was poison in his nostrils, every sound a cancer in the ears. I've been branded; and drowned by a king in heaven over the things I never thought I had done. Now I must confess to being branded by a devil's scar. One I will not be forgetting anytime soon. Faith is asking me to change even more of who I thought I was.

ROUND

This heart is falling asleep in a strange place. This icy wall we can't break through, and a fiery light burning the night. Measured only by the past fading away. Little orbs flutter about a room whispering their own ways home, and the depths we've reached into our cores. The division here is clear as circles have begun between the pawns, and crowns of rational thoughts. It focuses like a raindrop hitting water, and rippling out an echo in the mind. I have grown terrified of how empty handed this will leave me.

My faith responded;

"You are lucky to know miracles, and be aloud
to circle around given another chance."

I wander then in circles between a sun, and the long days of a heavy jaw sewn shut. Until I understand what I am supposed to do. Heaven hangs on a string now as he is living on the coffins and the dust. A past coughed up to send him another round of mistakes. He lost his faith somewhere worse off he did not notice it was slipping away. Angels have come to dance around him through the night giving relief to his swelling heart but his ears are empty. His lips are stitched shut.

ALCHEMY

I am here standing alone in my corner of the Earth. Singing along with the pain in my own heart. Loud enough to watch the day fall into the horizon and wash it all out to sea.

All I know is this alchemy has formed stars in pits

below, and I believe it will swallow me whole.

DEAD

Back from the depths of the dead! I found a heavy heart filled
with hurt, and heavy breathing. It was a month ago I slipped
into a mindset that sees them. I thought I knew hurt until I
saw ghosts and ghouls crying out as I became one of them.
The blind and fearless race to face the terror of facing him
is a sight only the dead could understand. Nothing is left
safe for a hidden wire guiding this light I'm holding.

The crashing then crumbling reality drags me further, and
further into the sea. I am begging to be thrown into the
rocks. Find a heaven that gives guidance to this living soul.
I know this madness does not show. but I am a body left
broken by the ethereal absorption melting my heart away.

An energetic being after the weather has moved in and crushed
the sounds of this body. The soul has woken to its glee to navigate
by sonar pings. Old thoughts are dead at this end, destroyed in
the breakwater never to be found. When the tide will pull the
corpses out to sea. I am not dead, but alive in the spirit coming
to change everything, still it shows we have a long way to go.

HARDENED

Write yourself down the wires into the hard part. The stalwart
self; and the enigma of a man sharing his world at total war.
Light up a cigar. The last one before the sunset on the horizon
fades into the dark. I cannot shake the thought that I will never
escape the sins I'm reaching over; and this war will find no end.

The faith that softens also hardens to leave sin; and bring
the present accountable through peeling off the scars.

I reaped and sewed death yesterday. I died in that place. I was toe-
tagged, forgiven, but not forgotten. That is what this faith claims.
You'll see my heart survived the flood while it was drowning.

It turned blacker than night itself and left just
a coal that is self-combustible.

Pressurized under faith; and formed in the beat red corners
of his eyes. Through that storm and flood, I am truly amazed
I survived; and it was not by my own doing I did. Those
feelings became pyroclastic flowing through sorrow and
anger. I am struggling to admit he has forgiven and hardened
me too face everything with a smile on this face.

WITHDRAWLS

I did not expect jumping in the water and putting out a
cigarette would leave me cast to sit beside a devil pretending
I've grown out of this haze. Imaginary senses all around;
and I try like a devil myself to survive escaping these things.
Stop listening to all the noises. The ones digging a grave
through these lungs I need the change in my lungs.

I was left slipping into the disguise of a devil, shown so clearly in
the sunspots of my burning eyes. I know this is no spiritual war,
but it certainly could be in a thirty second commercial trying
to change our minds on our toxic needs. The constant losing
and fighting is true as any other war waged. The longest days feel
like swallowing lead. Heavy rounds of torment. Blood lines are
drawn in the fog to prove the worth of cleaning this place. That
awful taste of stifling clouds blind the nose of the scent of rust.

In the end, I am still losing, but I am forgiven of even this
crime. I know a love that knows no boundaries in heaven,
but I cannot rationalize that as a good excuse.

SELF-DESTRUCTIVE

Hard fights are coming.

Moving forward in this destruction of who I am.

Telling this hand to take shape.

I know you well to play a game against my thoughts.

To flip, tap; and spin it around.

Sinking yourself into new eyes.

Inking out the things I never wanted to write,

because the fear is knocking at the mind.

Flipping. Tapping, and spinning around.

Finding myself becoming the one thing I never aimed for.
Blackened by mistakes. Without mercy, and a weaponized
pen. I laid my life into this destructiveness.

Here I am silencing the sound of warfare.

To bring heaven down.

Long after I greeted the dead.

I've learned to sort this out by,

flipping,

Tapping; and spinning around.

PREMONITIONS

Dense smoke warning.
Wandered deeper into darker wastes.
Outer worlds and memorials.
Gale force storms in a blink.

Between two frames.
At the birth of raw insanity.
Photos of burning things.
Lights in exoplanetary plains.

Revolutions of a cosmic leap.
Songs in a light acid rain.
A new mask rises.
Bone crunching escapes.

Heat waves and cold spells.
Woven in rotation.
Warring with machines.
Greet this feather weight light.
Everything is dead by the end of this long night.

WONDERLAND

I sense the shadows drifting on. Did they find someone better?
Was I pardoned of my mutiny? Will I wake, and live again? Something has changed this time. My hands still tremble as a voice
groans about my morning coffee. I am blaming the fragile control
over emotions; and the will to fight becoming iron-like. All the
while the morning light is wafting off the magic residue in the air.

I keep tucked away one more day for a certain clarity as
the little bird's song rewires a shattered frame. Reality is
long gone, and I know this madness well. I have my faith.
Always clinging onto that faith for survival. The sweat
stains dampen the page; and I turn into the wonderland of
his grace. Soon reality will rebound back. I cannot believe
my savior died so I could wander in this wonderful place.

BELIEF

I have a reason to fight in this battlefield. I will not stand
just a witness to a war on evil things. I know the belief
saturating my veins across the pages has turned into
a reality. True reality buried deep once has returned
to show how everything I am has changed.

The bloods metallic taste sinks in, and this time I will
confess with lips how I believe. How do I confess, I am
saved? I close my eyes in the darkness and the comfort of
prayer still sounds like incantations that ring loud where
bones glow and flesh melts. The branded palm burns black
and the pentagrams are flowing with wires deep into the
left half, while the right-side explodes with flight.

These things I once believed have grown far to weak to carry
further, I know now only one name is right, and we call him Jesus.

MOJAVE

Sandstorms and warm passing rain.

Summer monsoons bring a sweet smell.

Mojave's last relief before the mercury explodes.

A break from the boiling in my mind. Solid Earth floats in watery pools. Light-hearted days I have learned to cherish. With a waking eye absolutely mesmerized.

Survivor of doing things the hard way. Madness could stir the soul today. Then the smell of sweet rain takes my breath away. Days like today, will forever be welcome in this place.

The smell of swirling clouds seeping down. The cooling weather that wipes sweat patterns off his shirt. This weather reinforces a new peace in my mind. Bad luck means nothing. A new view on color born from a true faith.

A hope, I hope stays long after this monsoon is swept away.

One I hope to find when the triple digits break crack glass.

MIDNIGHT THOUGHTS

My dead arm quivers. Midnight alarm, and a flash of light across the dry lake. No sign of humans whatsoever. A sudden spin of confusion, and a heartbeat escalates that I might be on my way to going insane. An evil comes in through my down guarded dreaming this battle was finally won. Thought it was a calm night when talk radio brings reality home. I am indeed awake. They ramble on about problems in L.A. and all around the world stories of war are so far from home.

Step out and stare at midnight clouds. I am wondering if somewhere in the universe there is a continent that still resembles Pangea. With that thin layer of atmosphere above reminding me of a primordial bog; with islands, and borders strung around a half moon. While the glow draws the beauty out. The late-night thoughts on the tail end of a smoke, as I recover from a panic attack. I concede defeat in a stale cup of black coffee that I need one good night of sleep.

SIMPLER THOUGHTS

I am stuck in a realm of cupid playing messenger of heart
strings that fail to hit a tune. I'd ask kindly of Zeus to
fire him already all this back and forth is hurting; and I
would pay to watch Cupid fall as if he were Icarus.

Go back to your wife, you're drunk shooting at me. I
will admit; I fell in love with her story. I do not believe
she had a choice but fall from your grace and confront
your mother. (What a bitch to be sure.)

Just these little thoughts about a wonderful
story of the female Psyche.

TRIANGLES

There is a late-night breeze in my window. A mid-summer scorched Earth policy in full force, and a strange conversation between God and the Devil. I am stuck in between with the mystery of man.

Mankind itself, the topic of the two;

"I've no reason to corrupt this one's hell."

The other replies;

"I've no reason to bring the living dead to heaven."

I myself say;

"Can I just be allowed to sleep?"

No reply is given, as I no longer question these types of crazy things. I am wondering why they speak at all.

I have no reason to wander into heaven or hell.

BLINDNESS

When I was abducted, and/or visited by other worldly
feelings. Why did they remove one eye yet leave
the other blind? Did they forget I am still mortal
bound by blood, and seeing what I believe?

While they took my senses. I watched my share of the
Earth burn slowly into ash. I understand now I must
read the Bible to make sense of anything at all.

All this understanding spoken in an instant
blink of my missing eyes.

FIRE SHIPS

To sit in the flames where you fought the cold with all the passion a pen can summon. Silently burning every corner of your vessel sinking below. You'll find this wreckage of what was, once, a war. These pieces of soul still ignite the plank you walked on. The embers of a fuse burn slow and low. I only dive deep now to remember I have a soul. One reaching into the faith I had to create.

It still asks for war, and still begs for more; but I have learned a better way then casting fire ships her way.

An insanity taught him to love himself so much more then with reckless abandonment. It was never about our destruction, but the love we would find in who we were becoming. The compassion I found rose from the wreckage of the fires. The cold war may always beg us to give freely a little spark that becomes a fiery ship bound for death, and set to burn the sea apart.

CAPTIVE

I find a warmth in the scars of the love that captured stars.
It might take a lifetime putting them all back in place with
a fire to burn far beyond our bad timing. I found a belief in
something more then just what I see in front of my face.
That faith changed everything. It will forever mesmerize
me. It fills the morning sky when I wake with all these
thoughts that the sea is on fire, and yet I am safe.

Although the Fires eventually burn out.
Our faith does not cast us out.

STRANGEST THINGS

The two A.M. conversation with myself returns! Although I cannot find peace in sleep. There is a shadow playing peek-a-boo outside, and a bat hovering about on the window. A wide view of the universe fills with galaxies, and stretches across my living room. With all the colors and shapes imaginable creating a tree. My eyes are becoming the Hubble Telescope. A rocket ship passes through my kitchen into the center of the Milky Way; and it all disappears high into the night sky. Saturn has appeared as if standing on its own rings.

Am I asleep as I write these things? The two A.M. conversation has evolved into a pen dreaming while awake; and the atmosphere itself becomes a portrait into another world.

STOLEN PARTS

Now open the eyes to reborn fire in frozen blood.

I hope the best for you as Earth and hope runs asunder.

Stare at the rising of two suns filled with wild, and
flaring clarity in what you have done.

Look up across the clouds bringing a summer
rain that hides all our pain.

Then look deeper, and see the portraits we painted
reminding you of the love we gained.

Will you fall in a single breath with all your stolen parts?

Whispering secrets to the bee resting on your nose.

As it speaks of flowers ready to bloom.

That is the love of mankind unfolding in a moment.

I'd rather fold inward, and let you live but I know what
I stole is broken parts found among the dead.

VANITY

Fate itself is catching fire as we bleed; and
it burns until it burns us out.

Before we go to war; and show off our cold scars.

Our ashes are already fused among stars.

You and I already know how we believe in miracles
beginning; and we know how our lives end.

You face my way, and I turn to yours.

Will we find what we fell for this time?

We are trapped in the madness of our own vane hearts.

I made my decision. I am diving deeper to rip
open the sky we found in love.

That sky hiding the meaning in all things to
show why we wear these rings.

WOUNDS

Behind fort walls I've learned to laugh instead of
showing wounds that bloom Eden's gardens.

I still curse the cut and bare the weather that started
everything I've grown to love. Both the beauty; and the ugliest
of things I find in this place leave a raw and tender mark.

I came to give; and to give, means death.

Will you wash these wounds then drown them in salt
through the love of Eden's second bloom?

IMMUNE

I find that single word that defines my changing view on the world. I feel it as I fathom the wide cosmos; and the distance feet have moved across these pages. I locked the notions away in my mind summing up what it means to experience, yet never feel, or vice versa.

Like a day spent rolling through ash, brushing off burnt skin with charcoal set to ignite. The heavy heat of the day drives it all to burn in a madness I understand.

The smoke lines bring snow flurries; and deep chases into the interior of cold, frozen skin where stars linger buried away guiding a truth I cannot replace. A world that wraps itself around understanding life; and all the folds of a flowing river that smooths jagged stones. I felt deep into a core below the floor. An even deeper pouring down into the quantum and cosmic layers still pushing out against velvet, and cashmere.

Reality though is far different. I feel passive. I have grown immune to soft and tender. So, I tear at skin with dry stones.

JELLYFISH

Dive in headfirst straight to the bottom.

Bump the mind on bedrock; and take a spin
to make you say new things.

Hold a breath in, and peel the scales away with a raised hand.

Until we are seeing starlight in daylight; and jellyfish
float across eyesight.

Growing as big as clouds floating around
in words we found in them.

Filling the sea with color whispering around prettiest
things in a shadow.

Dance around the moonlight; and let them
reach down to pick you up.

In a hundred growing tentacles making us feel pins and needles.

All we can say then we will get them until all this is simple.

Laugh and love like magic to cast again and again.

CREATION

Shaking and shivering when Earth is cracking open
underfoot. I break clean apart for once into the depths of
creation. A late night in lost time trying to steady tremors
of an open heart. Soon it will calm instead of shake; and all
will be right for a night. I have grown used to this nauseous
disintegrating design of stepping into a garden.

Stepping up to a unsteady wheel to ease an unsteady
pressure . A passionate drive within the mind. Breath
deep to loosen the cramps of a swelling hand. Release
the soul that grows in a garden not built by sin.

I can smell the flow of creation stirring inside, and out.
An overpowering, neither hot nor cold pattern swirls
in the deep expansion of what is hidden in a rib.

For once, I admit this heart has a handle on an energetic
cognitive thought igniting joy.

ZIPPO

Bring fire again across these pages before I find my good luck charm; and burn a name off every note. Burn every page for simply mentioning you. It is a self-gratifying need, and a satisfying greed feeding the monstrous heart through flesh bound eyes exchanging mortal life for immortal notions. A backwards logic to admit heaven starts in hell. We all start somewhere at the bottom to work our way back to life. I've seen everything now. I swallowed fire where I lost control of my own being. I've seen the hurricane arise from the ash a million times over. A storm coming like a meteor strike that brings an ice age into focus and the end of monstrosities living in the mind.

I am letting loose the grudge; and hate that barricaded me behind closed doors. The prison cells where I cannot see the stars. I am holding a good luck charm in my hand while saying a prayer to come back stronger than the shell of a mortal man. I am going to step out and light these pages on fire to see what is real in this life. The hollow caverns won't be found. Ever. My will to run will win. It will search for proof that life is more then good luck charms, and prayers. Maybe I just need to see that this zippo still works, but I will be satisfied for the first time in the longest time.

THE BEAST

I challenge a beast today in the mental permutation of reality
collapsing overhead. A changing in the fractured thoughts.
A healing in the ones that no longer hold sway in chaos.

I have lost my senses to the beast who owns a contaminated
space. So very cold and nearly absolute zero, in that
dead place. A cold that knows no motion. Still the
burn lingers far from where I sleep at night.

Earth herself has cried heresy when I thought I'd be
convicted by the tongue of a mans shambling feet.

The beast is burning underneath this disease
that curses what I feel in my sleep.

JUNGLES

The jungle will breathe its weight casting life out among vine and feather to become decay among the leaves.

I've tasted both sweet pine and honey liquor through jungles of heartbeats and an untamed art.

My engine of death has grown still but roars up from the depths when my guard slips.

Chaos runs this place at an arm's length when I reach for the vine and unfreeze a cold lonely night.

It has become feathers I've learned I miss the most. That time when I was not alone. Long before fighting mirrors become a hobby; and I learned how to hold scars close.

It's the same vine and feather that reach into the law of the jungle allowed to have its way with you.

SLIVERS

Into triple digits. The sun jumps across the sky. Fiery hell to those roaming to close. While the psyche wanders Neptune. Deep in dark blue oceans and heavy winds I feel.

Does Pluto know of either and how judgment is a sliver.

I slip into the daydream on the water off a little pier, breathing slower; and taking my secrets to the grave of a pen. I have met him, Pluto I mean.

A grey thin man with devil horns hiding in his moustache. He went off searching for this light; and while my face went white, he found it in an underworld brought of life. As the dead stumble on their feet, a cold dead corpse is rising heavy in its beats and symmetry. A devil stole a soul and watered the blood with slivers in our feet.

Time to forget what I have seen. Start again, and bleed clean as gold. My enemy is alive; and I am swearing denial from this day forward. Filling this cup with grace and love. As slivers are pulled from my hands and feet.

KITCHEN DUTY

I am going to war with my kitchen. Neck deep in three-
week old dead rotten fleshy gunk, spewing behind
enemy lines. Between a clean fresh sink and I, stands
armies of pig fat and molten beef bone.

"Over the top!" I cheer. Armed with a sponge and a jet of fiery
faucet spray. The layers of death vaporize; and peel away in the
foul rising odor of victory pouring my way. Ambushed by an
even stronger pungent smell choking the bottom of my lungs.

"Gas, gas, gas!" I holler across the room, and tremble struggling
to breath. This is the bottom of the sink where all death and
decay now lay. I re-arm with a new weapon, steel wool.

I threw it into the storm while scolding hot water,
soap and bubbles erupt into my blinded eyes. I dove
back into the trenches and blasted away what remains
of death with a water infused flamethrower.

"Victory!"

SKIES

As low as this frame goes in empty minded thoughts. A
stretching clock; and memories still hide in the tides that
bump my head off.. Through a water box and moving
compasses track nothing past the desert moon where I
once watched a hangman's noose. You'll jump until your
blue, and crystalline coffins sooth the salted wounds. You'll
dream of snow in summer and still dream of it in winter.

Watching a star fall from the sky tonight. I asked what happened
as I lost my mind. He began chasing an end of this universe
and he'll find it just as he is knocked back to Earth. No longer
wearing a blue. I was only wondering what it was worth to
steal a horse, in a town they might still hang you for it. San
Quentin would be a good answer, but they'll hang you for it.

MY WINDOW

I could appeal to the laws of men asking for forgiveness
I'd never receive. Time is making it hard to run from an
empty room filled with a sky. I sense growth and see it give
new portraits in the clouds outside the window teaching
us where to go. I've burned so thoroughly for mistakes
searching among the elements for where that star fell. That
trip across the starry skies left a scar worth being the change
and I cannot account for it being of this Earth. Far into this
mystery I've been pulled from my comfort zones.

When I return, remind me I am bound by Earthly body still
human and moving forward into a beautiful azure.

FLASHBACKS

Torment and agony still linger solid in my mind of two worlds.
Two broken heartbeats that cannot sing. Holding orbit for
weeks then months; and it may be years until we recover from
what broke us. Praying to never become a unsympathetic
energy bound by empathy. Still if it is to be then a stalwart
paragon of pentagrams exists. (Oh, how I have changed.)

Challenging death in words while stepping out into the cold
frozen oblivions between hellfire, and hallucinations that
swallow heartbeats and minds whole. (Oh, how I have changed.)

A change to his steady years on calm seas a cold crusader
of a type of freedom.

I have said goodbye to Olympus and Hades. I will find
myself lost in time and silent recovery. Where hands
reach into the soul I regained. Through it, heaven
has become a feeling beyond imagination.

NOSTALGIA

Through color and light after long dark nights. The flashbacks, and a new life. I smile in nostalgic memories. This is a whisper of love into the cool air. I've taken a seat high on my island under that old swaying tree grown across the cosmos holding everything in place. It's arms alone could light up the night with amazing things.

The leaves have grown into galaxies seen reaching further then yesterday. All of it bound together by grape vines of translucent light. With all the auroras and nebulas both above and below stretching beyond the sight. The frozen peaks in the distance of the mountains we overcame hide the setting suns dim reflection across a crystal-clear glacial lake. Calm and still wrapping around our feet.

MEMORIES

This place of memory and all the reflections of life. I'll be holding close through the aging years. When these war drums strike their last beat, and the rain no longer resembles blood in sand strewn across an arena. I will return here. I'll cross the distance among the waves and the winds to find the pulse of this place. Beyond the storms that hide it away. I'll overtake the fevers that leave death in the wake. Step into rhythm with living color that was hidden from my hands. Two sides of paradise have joined in this view to remember.

FROZEN

Once you find a dream of a soothing sea; and drown into
the calm water you believe in something bigger. At
least I have. You can imagine anything in the universe
at your fingertips. Every star, every galaxy and color of
the cosmos stirs in the palette of light you choose.

Frozen peaks swell above clouds for you to climb looking like
some distant frozen world. The snow has come to clean out
this memory I made. The glow of stars glisten below ready to
go back above. Everything I've come to know will soon freeze
and fall silently away becoming one more part of the whole.

Each is named as the old blue moon retakes the ground I stole.
Soon even the sun will be alone though it may always exist in his
burning veins. Soon it will all be a frozen place forgotten. It will
light the darkness and her worth will be written in stone. Though
long gone when these stories are told. Steadier in the cold, calm
enough to stop, and watch life unfold as it grows. As the nebulas
start spinning slowing moving further away into the dust.

EXPLORE

Time to explore that love. Let it sink. As it crumbles and melts into meaning. The soul unfolds by chills that once meant a breakdown until exploring love becomes simple. Until it becomes an endless flood of time and air burning through the lungs. The cold ocean can greet the moon on the opposite coast. Here I'll greet it with a sunrise. A cratered landscape becoming that tree she whispers around. It only begins here while my questions burn around a suit of flesh and bone.

Time to admit the habit I found is swallowing me again; and I am on the run to the love I hold in life. The pen lit up the room and the daylight war wages on and on to see what two can do. I just want to explore. Give admission to myself to admit I need her more then the words and sights I hear.

Their shadows reach the sea yet never show the bottom anymore. Shimmering water from the land we melted has frozen. Faith in God has grown. In my belief, I am so grateful to have found a way to describe something incredible in the craters of my soul. In that faith, I concede God himself is the cradle of life.

LOVE

Run my hands across her skin like feathers gently gliding into a heavenly place. Let me explore your hair and this new halo you claim. I went mad yesterday to fall into this love. This time dead and cold has absolutely no place between us. I'll be exploring you without words. I'll press my lips against a sweet sweat soaked desperation to create a love full of mercy and grace in smoother strokes. Molten roots became iron holes for keys. I am made to turn this into trust; and whatever love may come.

Dig deep or fly away. The Earth has moved us close and choked us up. Not this time, not tonight. We are driving nails into our graves. From the lips, and down into the hips. The hands stretched out scattering stardust on your skin. I am sadistic in the sounds you create bleeding off chemicals into foreign atmospheres to be here. How human of you to need Earth's approval. Lay back and feel it spin awhile because I approve of you.

Sickness may swell and steal what we create, but I know we have the strength to find what remains.

TIME

The universe is whispering it is time. We need to fade away.
I could pray love will bring us back, but the clock is ticking
silently now as even you and I must fall back into place.

The breeze still blows to cool our flesh instead of torturing
our brains. Thunderheads move close but never reach
the porch. I think you and I are climbing on the hands of
a clock fighting against the motion of the Earth.

The same storms that moved my love across the cosmos pulled
my heart back into my chest and it will be lost to time and space.
A solid, and Earthly existence has come to take its place. Sitting
beside something bigger than I could ever rationalize. Time has
opened; and closed the door on us. The truth no longer hurts.
I've saved our memory in a safe place that will never change.

It's time to heal all the wounds time to let people fade; and
time to remember we cannot forget what built our faith.

The scars might become your war tomorrow. A mental
illness with no certainty of when it'll explode over you.
Remember what you are fighting for is a silent truth.

VIEWS

Funniest day of my life occurred as I woke up just a light in a void when I thought it faded. I stopped using my eyes. I tried to move slower but only went speeding forward. Read this world by warmth, and chills in my chest. The ones that eventually sink into the pits. They leave us darker than darkness itself. I remember the things we pretended could exist. The lovers sky; and all the feelings wired through us. We both searched for an imagination to view life. We found only the swelling sea and crashed into the deep.

I miss her again in the early hours before sunrise. I sit quiet with my coffee brewing and close my eyes in prayers. I am holding onto the closest thing to art I found. I plunge further into faith to realize I have only begun a journey across time and space. I grip tighter on the book I started reading. The sharp sting settles in that I have finally accepted this to tame the beast. I fold these little notes into paper planes, and throw them out the window before I hit save. A few survive with a better view.

I was hoping they would fly home. and get lost wherever they came from because I've learned to love the answer to; "Who am I?"

PRIVATE INFORMATION

A definition I found of soul has become a public piece; and bound outside my bones by private conflicts. Conflicts the ink can only share at the surface. I have only one goal in life to share the love of a fiery star. A jewel in the sky that landed in a sapphire heart. A fire I carry in my hands. The only piece of a body I've found to be both private and public in it's creativity. The hand of man that waves a pen across the window staring into a jungle; and staring beyond the abyss. The conflicts wouldn't be private if I had my way but the imagery lost in the mind is beyond the jungles; and beyond rational thinking. I am just another artist lost sharing the love of a star holding Earth captive.

THE END

Follow the tears into the notes crumpled on the floor. Stand
straight up and slide out the door. Turn the keys you hold to
your own mind. Wonderful things exist. I believe the worth
of the human spirit. I am lost in less sleep then you could
ever wish to feel comfortable. Loosen up your will to control
and all those expectations of this place will float away.

Tear into the bones with a smile. Fight against the
ocean waves until the ground solidifies below. Don't
forget the aftershocks from the first falls. The lightning
and thunder follows close when you have years ahead
to search below. Remember, let them all float.

Goosebumps settle at the bottom of my minds little drain
to walk away from all of this. When it all disappears and
you're at the journey's end, I hope you look back to say;

"This life will always be beautiful; and everything will be okay."

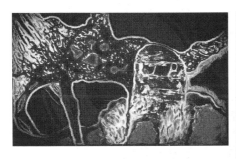

AUTUMN

Dance and sway into the night. And we'll grind through the days creating dreamers escapes until we become them. All it takes is in our dance. Keep on dancing us through our lover's escapade. Your prayers speak volumes louder then just slipping into you like a new best suit. You've got more then chess on your mind; and I am holding onto one thought...Dancing with you.

Burn this body. Time is senseless. Time is collapsing. I have passed through so many cities searching. I'm coming for you now. I'll be there soon. I will be there dancing with you.

Finding our words that burn the whole damn system down. Our way you say? Lovers that glow Lovers that dance and sway.

All the best stars already know; and traded it all in for the color of a satellite screen.

Burn this body into building the shape and shift of our realities. Moving forward in ours has me setting fire the sun. Setting fire to the solar flares in memory.

About Joshua Wells

Joshua Wells was born in Downey, CA on September 5th, 1986. Growing up all over Southern California. He began writing poetry at the age of 16 without a college education and living on small jobs here and there. He spent a brief time in Northern California where his daughter Sydney Mae Wells was born on July 4th,2008. Following a bad breakup he begin his journey to become a full time author. That journey took him across 40 States inspiring a life for Christ and a pursuit for all forms of truth and happiness.

Made in the USA
Columbia, SC
29 May 2021